S0-DQV-580

Rebecca Donnelly   illustrated by **Misa Saburi**

How Slippery is a Banana Peel?

Have a Great day♥

GODWINBOOKS

Henry Holt and Company · New York

Volcanoes **roar**,
but banana peels race.

Rockets **soar** like bananas through space.

Is the moon a banana? What keeps it in place?

**Jellies wobble,
but banana peels swish.**

Hatchlings squabble,
but banana peels squish.

Do banana peels shine like the scales on a fish?

Roller coasters climb, but banana peels cling.

Eggs fall,
but banana peels fling.

Can banana-peel catapults sling everything?

**Lemons light,
but banana peels leap.**

You fly a kite,
but banana peels creep.

Is a squid a banana that dives in the deep?

Pennies sink,
but banana peels sail.

Bubbles float,
but banana peels flail.

Do banana slugs slide slower than a snail?

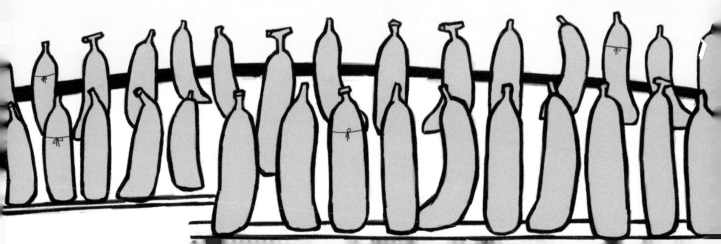

Seedlings drink,
but banana peels ooze.

Crystals clink,
but banana peels cruise.

Do rotting bananas smell worse than my shoes?

In conclusion,
banana peels whoosh.

We've measured the mess
when their insides go sloosh.

Some banana peels split,

but others go **splat**.

Hey, **watch out!**

Be careful!
Don't step on that!

What makes banana peels so slippery?

Imagine sliding across a smooth tile floor in your socks. *Whoosh!* Now imagine trying it on a carpeted floor—uh-oh. Why can we slip and slide on smooth surfaces but not as easily on rough ones? There's something at work here called *friction*. Friction is the force that resists movement between two surfaces—your socks and the floor, or your skates on the ice, or an empty banana peel and the sidewalk. There is low friction between your sock-covered feet and a smooth tile floor, and there's high friction between your socks and a carpet.

The well-known slip-and-slide properties of banana peels come from a gooey substance known as *polysaccharide follicular gel*. But the slipperiness of follicular gel isn't just good for laughs. Researchers are studying the goop to see if a human-made version can be used to lubricate artificial joints. Our joints are surrounded by sacs of fluid that allow them to move smoothly. The fluid, known as *synovial fluid,* reduces the friction as the bones in our joints move against one another.

Banana peels aren't the only things that make good use of slimy goop to lower friction. The banana slug (a mollusk native to the redwood forests of California and the Pacific Northwest) is not only shaped like a banana and often bright yellow in color, but it also produces a gooey substance to make movement easier as it travels along the forest floor and to keep it from dehydrating.

Read about the scientific paper that started it all!

Like anyone, scientists love a good joke. Japanese scientist Kiyoshi Mabuchi and his team measured the amount of friction between a banana peel and a plate covered in linoleum. Then, they measured the friction using different types of fruit, including apple and tangerine peels. You can learn more here: https://www.jstage.jst.go.jp/article/trol/7/3/7_147/_pdf

Activity

Zip line

You can make a simple zip line, using all kinds of materials, to explore how friction affects speed. Try the following experiment, and then see if you can use other materials to increase or decrease the friction on your zip line.

Materials

- 2 large paper clips
- Tape
- Small paper cup
- Action figure or other adventurous toy (small enough to fit inside the cup)
- Fishing line (at least 4 feet)

Directions

Unfold one paper clip completely and bend it so it forms a handle. Slide the other paper clip onto the clip you just unfolded. This will be your hook. Tape the ends of the unfolded paper clip to the paper cup. Put your toy inside the cup. Tie one end of the fishing line to the back of a chair, or tape it to a wall. You can tie the other end to something lower, weighing it down with a heavy object, or get someone to hold it for you. Hook your paper-clip-and-cup contraption onto the fishing line and watch it zip! You can change this experiment by making the zip line steeper or less steep, using something else like string or yarn for the line, or using something else for the hook. How do these changes affect the speed? Which materials create more friction?

For Julia, who never slips up —R. D.

**To all the excellent banana-bread-recipe creators
for making brown, squishy bananas desirable** —M. S.

Henry Holt and Company, *Publishers since 1866*
Henry Holt® is a registered trademark of Macmillan Publishing Group, LLC
120 Broadway, New York, NY 10271
mackids.com

Library of Congress Control Number: 2020910176
ISBN 978-1-250-25686-7
Our books may be purchased in bulk for promotional, educational, or business use.
Please contact your local bookseller or the Macmillan Corporate and Premium Sales Department
at (800) 221-7945 ext. 5442 or by email at MacmillanSpecialMarkets@macmillan.com.

First edition, 2021 / Design by Liz Dresner
All illustrations were drawn in Adobe Photoshop.
Printed in China by RR Donnelley Asia Printing Solutions Ltd.,
Dongguan City, Guangdong Province

1 3 5 7 9 10 8 6 4 2